# The Dinosaur's Packed Lunch

www.**randomhousechildrens**.co.uk

**COLOUR FIRST READER** books are perfect for beginner readers. All the text inside this Colour First Reader book has been checked and approved by a reading expert, so it is the ideal size, length and level for children learning to read.

*Also available in Colour First Reader:*

THE MONSTER STORY-TELLER
by Jacqueline Wilson

# Jacqueline Wilson
# The Dinosaur's Packed Lunch

Illustrated by Nick Sharratt

CORGI PUPS

THE DINOSAUR'S PACKED LUNCH
A CORGI PUPS BOOK 978 0 552 56480 9

First published in Great Britain by Doubleday,
an imprint of Random House Children's Publishers UK
A Random House Group Company

Doubleday edition published 1995
First Corgi Pups edition published 1996
Corgi Pups edition reissued 2008

This edition published 2011

5 7 9 10 8 6

Text copyright © Jacqueline Wilson, 1995
Illustrations copyright © Nick Sharratt, 1996

The right of Jacqueline Wilson to be identified as the author
of this work has been asserted in accordance with the
Copyright, Designs and Patents Act 1988.

Penguin Random House is committed to a sustainable future for our business,
our readers and our planet. This book is made from
Forest Stewardship Council® certified paper.

MIX
Paper from
responsible sources
FSC    FSC® C018179
www.fsc.org

Set in Bembo Infant MT Standard

Corgi Pups Books are published by Random House Children's Publishers UK,
61–63 Uxbridge Road, London W5 5SA

www.randomhousechildrens.co.uk
www.randomhouse.co.uk

Addresses for companies within The Random House Group Limited
can be found at: www.randomhouse.co.uk/offices.htm

THE RANDOM HOUSE GROUP Limited Reg. No. 954009

A CIP catalogue record for this book is available
from the British Library.

Printed in China

*For Bunny, with lots of love*

# CONTENTS

Series Reading Consultant: Prue Goodwin
Reading and Language Information Centre,
University of Reading

# Chapter One

Dinah woke up early.

She didn't feel like getting washed. She didn't feel like getting dressed. She didn't feel like going to school.

"Boring," said Dinah.

Dinah did not feel like
breakfast.

Not cornflakes and milk.

"Boring," said Dinah.

She made herself a jam
sandwich.

"Yummy," said Dinah,
rubbing her tummy.

She fed the teddy on her
nightie, too.

Dinah wanted a drink but the lemonade was right at the top of the cupboard with Dad's beer.

Dinah couldn't reach.

Then she saw Dad's window-cleaning ladder.

Dinah nearly reached the lemonade.

But then the ladder slipped.

Dad woke up early, too.

Dinah hated it when Dad got cross. She didn't have a mum or any brothers or sisters. Dinah just had her dad.

"How am I going to clean the windows now?" said Dad. "And take that thumb out of your mouth, baby."

Dinah always sucked her thumb when she was sad. Her special sucking thumb was starting to get a bit pointed.

Dinah was still sucking her thumb when she went to school. The boys teased her. Dinah got cross. There was a fight.

Then Miss Smith got cross and sent Dinah indoors.

Dinah had a little wash.
Dinah's best friend, Judy,
ended up having a little wash,
too.

Miss Smith got very cross and
said Dinah wouldn't go on the
school trip to the museum if she
wasn't careful.

"A museum?" Dinah muttered.
"Boring."

Dinah's best friend, Judy, was still very damp. She didn't feel like sitting next to Dinah on the minibus. She sat next to Danielle, and they kept giggling together.

Dinah had to sit next to Miss Smith.

When they got to the
museum Judy went off arm in
arm with Danielle.

"I don't care," said Dinah,
sucking her thumb.

## Chapter Two

Dinah cheered up when they went into a special dinosaur exhibition. Dinosaurs were huge monsters who lived millions of years ago.

Dinah liked the look of dinosaurs.

Some of the dinosaurs were very fierce and vicious. Judy and Danielle squealed. Dinah didn't mind a bit.

The dinosaurs had huge long names to match their size.

Dinah wasn't very good at reading but she found she had no problem spelling out brontosaurus . . .

. . . and tyrannosaurus and triceratops.

She particularly liked the
iguanodon. It had a funny
pointed thumb spike. Perhaps the
iguanadon sucked
its thumb, too.

Miss Smith got cross because
Dinah kept lagging behind.

"Hurry up, Dinah. It's
lunchtime," said Miss Smith.

Everyone had a packed lunch except Dinah. Dad always forgot things like packed lunches. Sometimes Judy shared her packed lunch with Dinah. But not today.

"Ooh, my mum's given me prawn sandwiches and a bunch of grapes and a Kit Kat and a can of Coke. Want half my Kit Kat, Danielle?" said Judy.

Dinah crept away, feeling
very empty. She wandered back
to the iguanodon, sucking her
thumb.

"I wish I had a mum to make
me a packed lunch," said Dinah.

A hand reached out and
patted her on the shoulder.

A huge scaly hand with a
spiked thumb!

22

The iguanodon reached down
and picked Dinah up. It cradled
her in its arms, rocking
backwards and forwards.

The iguanodon made Dinah her own packed lunch.

She ate a leaf sandwich, a bunch of daisies, a twig snack bar and a bottle of dinosaur juice.

The dinosaur juice was a very bright green. It tasted strange too, but Dinah drank a few drops.

The iguanodon wiped Dinah's mouth in a motherly way.

"Dinah! Where *are* you?"

Miss Smith was coming! Dinah jumped down and the iguanodon shot back into place with a rattle and a clunk. Miss Smith didn't see. She was cross with Dinah.

Dinah was too dazed to care.

All the other children were in the gift shop buying books and stickers and little rubber dinosaurs.

Dinah didn't have any money but she didn't mind. She didn't want a book or a sticker or a little rubber dinosaur.

She had just had a dinosaur's packed lunch!

Dinah was very quiet on the bus going back.

"You're not going to be sick, are you, Dinah?" Miss Smith asked anxiously.

Dinah wasn't sure. She felt very strange. She sucked her thumb, but it tasted strange, too.

She went to bed straight after supper. Perhaps she should have had a bath. Her skin felt strange now, hard and dry and itchy.

29

Dinah sucked her strange thumb and went to sleep. She dreamt very strange dreams.

## Chapter Three

When Dinah woke, something
even stranger had happened.

She sat up and her head
bumped against the ceiling! Her
bed was so tiny she had to cram
her knees right up under her chin.

Her bedroom had shrunk in
the night.

No. Even stranger . . .

Dinah had grown. She had
grown and grown and grown.
She had grown a long back and
long legs and a long tail!

Dinah gasped and sucked her thumb. At least she still *had* a thumb.

She wondered what to do.

She decided she'd better tell Dad.

She had to bend double to get out of her bedroom door and . . .

edge along the hall, her head
neatly sweeping up the cobwebs
(Dinah and her dad didn't
bother about dusting) . . .

and then she had to bend right
down again to get into Dad's
bedroom.

"Dad. Dad! Wake up, Dad,"
said Dinah.

"What's the matter?" Dad
mumbled. "Stop yelling at me,
Dinah."

Dad peered out from under
the bedcovers. He saw Dinah.

Dad was the one who did the
yelling this time.

"Aaaaaaaaah!"

"A monster! A monster! Run, Dinah, there's a monster in my bedroom," Dad yelled.

"Hey, Dad. It's me, Dinah. I'm the monster," said Dinah. "Well, I think I've turned into a dinosaur, actually. It feels a bit scary. Give me a cuddle, Dad."

It was a bit scary for Dad, too. But he could see the huge dinosaur in his bedroom was wearing Dinah's nightie and talking with Dinah's voice.

It was his daughter Dinah all right. So he gave her a cuddle as best he could.

Then Dinah gave Dad a cuddle, which was much easier. It was fun being able to pick Dad up with her new arms. She'd have to remember to cut her claws though.

Her new skin didn't need a
wash but her arms ached when
she cleaned all her new teeth
with Dad's big clothes-brush.

Dinah was terribly greedy at breakfast. She ate a whole loaf of bread in one gollop and finished a jar of jam with one lick.

"Well, I'm a growing girl," said Dinah, giggling.

"I don't know how I'm going to afford to feed you now. Money doesn't grow on trees," said Dad.

Luckily, Dinah liked eating
trees. Well, the leaves and the
smaller snappier branches. And
privet hedges taste delicious if
you're a dinosaur.

Everyone got their hedges
trimmed and their trees pruned
for nothing.

## Chapter Four

Dad took Dinah to the doctor's.

"Can you cure my Dinah?" asked Dad.

"I think you'd better take her to a vet," said the doctor.

Dinah did a bit of doctoring herself.

She cured a baby's hiccups and made an old lady's bad leg better.

Dad took Dinah to the vet's.
"Well, she's certainly got a
healthy appetite," said the vet.
"I don't think there's anything
wrong with her."

"In that case you'd better go
to school," said Dad.

"Boring," said Dinah.

But maybe school might be
more fun today.

She certainly caused a bit of
fuss when she went in through
the school gates.

Dad had to have a few words with Miss Smith.

Miss Smith wasn't at all sure she could cope with this new Dinah.

"It's OK, Miss Smith. I'll be ever so good," said Dinah.

Dinah did try to be good. She didn't talk in the (now very crowded) class, but when she started to get bored she gave her new long tail a little flick . . .

which caused a bit of bother . . .

and at playtime she fought the
boys . . .

and splashed the girls BUT . . .

she somehow didn't get into
trouble.

Everyone wanted to play with Dinah now.

"Dinah's my best friend," said Judy.

"I'll be best friends with everyone," said Dinah. "Hey, who wants a ride on my tail?"

"Dinah's better than Disneyland!" said Judy.

Dinah even gave Miss Smith
a ride!

When Dad collected her from
school, Dinah helped him clean
all the windows in the street.

People paid
double to watch
Dad climb up and
down his new
ladder.

Dinah and Dad got very hot working so hard.

"Let's go home and have a cool bath," said Dad.

"Boring," said Dinah. "Let's go swimming."

So Dinah and Dad went to
the swimming pool. There wasn't
much pool left after Dinah
dived in!

Dinah made an excellent
diving board and water fountain.

It took Dad a very long time
to get her properly dry.

Dad had fish and chips for supper.

Dinah had leaves and privet and dandelions and nettles and long grass and a big bunch of flowers *and* fish and chips.

"Yummy," said Dinah, rubbing her tummy.

Dad tried his best to tuck her up in bed.

Dinah sucked her new spiked thumb until she fell asleep and . . .

when she woke up she was a
little girl again.

"Boring," said Dinah.

But she still had a nearly full
bottle of dinosaur juice . . .

THE END

Jacqueline Wilson is one of Britain's bestselling contemporary authors, with 30 million books sold in the UK. She has been honoured with many major prizes for her work, including the Guardian Children's Fiction Award and the Children's Book of the Year. She is the author most often borrowed from libraries over the last decade.

Jacqueline is a former Children's Laureate, a professor of children's literature and in 2008 she was appointed a Dame for services to children's literacy.

Nick Sharratt knew from an early age that he wanted to use his drawing skills as his career, so he went to Manchester Polytechnic to do an Art Foundation course. He followed this up with a BA (Hons) in Graphic Design at St Martin's School of Art in London from 1981 to 1984.

Since graduating, Nick has worked full-time as an illustrator for children's books, publishers and magazines. His brilliant illustrations have brought to life many books, most notably the titles by Jacqueline Wilson.

Nick also writes books as well as illustrating them.

# SLEEPOVERS

Amy, Bella, Chloe, Daisy and Emily
are friends at school and have their
own Alphabet Club (just look at their
initials!). The girls love having
sleepover parties for their birthdays.

But Daisy is worried – soon it
will be her turn. What will her friends
say when they meet her very
special big sister?

# LIZZIE ZIPMOUTH

Lizzie refuses to speak. She doesn't
want to talk to her new stepbrothers,
Rory and Jake, or her new stepdad,
Sam, or even her mum. Nothing at
all can make her change her mind.

But Lizzie's about to meet another
member of her new family who is
just as quiet as Lizzie – Great-Gran.
And she is even more stubborn!

# THE MONSTER STORY-TELLER

One morning at school, Natalie is very bored. Then she has a big surprise – there is a tiny monster at the window, waving at her! Suddenly Natalie's day is about to become much more exciting . . .

They whizz off together for some monster fun, and soon Natalie has lots of special stories to tell!

**COLOUR FIRST READER**